KALITAN OUR LITTLE ALASKAN COUSIN

MARY F. NIXON ROULET

Kalitan Our Little Alaskan Cousin

CHAPTER I

KALITAN TENAS

IT was bitterly cold. Kalitan Tenas felt it more than he had in the long winter, for then it was still and calm as night, and now the wind was blowing straight in from the sea, and the river was frozen tight.

A month before, the ice had begun to break and he had thought the cold was over, and that the all too short Alaskan summer was at hand. Now it was the first of May, and just as he had begun to think of summer pleasures, lo! a storm had come which seemed to freeze the very marrow of his bones. However, our little Alaskan cousin was used to cold and trained to it, and would not dream of fussing over a little snow-storm.

Kalitan started out to fish for his dinner, and though the snow came down heavily and he had to break through the ice to make a fishing-hole, and soon the ice was a wind-swept plain where even his own tracks were covered with a white pall, he fished steadily on. He never dreamed of stopping until he had fish enough for dinner, for, like most of his tribe, he was persevering and industrious.

Kalitan was a Thlinkit, though, if you asked him, he would say he was "Klinkit." This is a tribe which has puzzled wise people for a long time, for the Thlinkits are not Esquimos, not Indians, not coloured people, nor whites. They are the tribes living in Southeastern Alaska and along the coast. Many think that a long, long time ago, they came from Japan or some far Eastern country, for they look something like the Japanese, and their language has many words similar to Japanese in it.

Perhaps, long years ago, some shipwrecked Japanese were cast upon the coast of Alaska, and, finding their boats destroyed and the land good to live in, settled there, and thus began the Thlinkit tribes.

The Chilcats, Haidahs, and Tsimsheans are all Thlinkits, and are by far the best of the brown people of the Northland. They are honest, simple, and kind, and more intelligent than the Indians living farther north, in the colder regions. The Thlinkit coast is washed by the warm current from the Japan Sea, and it is not much colder than Chicago or Boston, though the winter is a little longer.

Kalitan fished diligently but caught little. He was warmly clad in sealskin; around his neck was a white bearskin ruff, as warm as toast, and very pretty, too, as soft and fluffy as a lady's boa. On his feet were moccasins of walrus hide. He had been perhaps an hour watching the hole in the ice, and knelt there so still that he looked almost as though he were frozen. Indeed, that was what those thought who saw him there, for suddenly a dog-sledge came round the corner of the hill and a loud halloo greeted his ears.

"Boston men," he said to himself as he watched them, "lost the trail."

They had indeed lost the trail, and Ted Strong had begun to think they would never find it again.

Chetwoof, their Indian guide, had not talked very much about it, but lapsed into his favourite "No understan'," a remark he always made when he did not want to answer what was said to him.

Ted and his father were on their way from Sitka to the Copper River. Mr. Strong was on the United States Geological Survey, which Ted knew meant that he had to go all around the country and poke about all day among rocks and mountains and glaciers. He had come with his father to this far Alaskan clime in the happiest expectation of adventures with bears and Indians, always dear to the heart of a boy.

He was pretty tired of the sledge, having been in it since early morning, and he was cold and hungry besides; so he was delighted when the dogs stopped and his father said:

"Hop out, son, and stretch your legs. We'll try to find out where we are before we go any farther."

Chetwoof meanwhile was interviewing the boy, who came quickly toward them.

"Who are you?" demanded Chetwoof.

"Kalitan Tenas," was the brief reply.

"Where are we?" was the next question.

"Near to Pilchickamin River."

"Where is a camp?"

"There," said the boy, pointing toward a clump of pine-trees. "Ours."

Ted by this time was tired of his own unwonted silence, and he came up to Kalitan, holding out his hand.

"My name is Ted Strong," he said, genially, grinning cheerfully at the young Alaskan. "I say this is a jolly place. I wish you would teach me to fish in a snow-hole. It must be great fun. I like you; let's be friends!" Kalitan took the boy's hand in his own rough one.

"Mahsie" (thank you), he said, a sudden quick smile sweeping his dark face like a fleeting sunbeam, but disappearing as quickly, leaving it grave again. "Olo?" (hungry).

"Yes," said Mr. Strong, "hungry and cold."

"Camp," said Kalitan, preparing to lead the way, with the hospitality of his tribe, for the Thlinkits are always ready to share food and fire with any stranger. The two boys strode off together, and Mr. Strong could scarcely help smiling at the contrast between them.

Ted was the taller, but slim even in the furs which almost smothered him, leaving only his bright face exposed to the wind and weather. His hair was a tangle of yellow curls which no parting could ever affect, for it stood straight up from his forehead like a golden fleece; his mother called it his aureole. His skin was fair as a girl's, and his eyes as big and blue as a young Viking's; but the Indian boy's locks were black as ink, his skin was swarthy, his eyes small and dark, and his features that strange mixture of the Indian, the Esquimo, and the Japanese which we often see in the best of our Alaskan cousins.

Boys, however, are boys all the world over, and friendly animals, and Ted was soon chattering away to his newly found friend as if he had known him all his life.

"What's your name?" he asked.

"Kalitan," was the answer. "They call me Kalitan Tenas; my father was Tyee."

"Where is he?" asked Ted. He wanted to see an Indian chief.

"Dead," said Kalitan, briefly.

"I'm sorry," said Ted. He adored his own father, and felt it was hard on a boy not to have one.

"He was killed," said Kalitan, "but we had blood-money from them," he added, sternly.

"What's that?" asked Ted, curiously.

"Long time ago, when one man kill another, his clan must pay with a life. One must be found from his tribe to cry, 'O-o-o-o-o-a-ha-a-ich-klu-kuk-ich-klu-kuk'" (ready to die, ready to die). His voice wailed out the mournful chant, which was weird and solemn and almost made Ted shiver. "But now," the boy went on, "Boston men" (Americans) "do not like the blood-tax, so the murderer pays money instead. We got many blankets and baskets and moneys for Kalitan Tyee. He great chief."

"Do you live here?" asked Ted.

"No, live on island out there." Kalitan waved his hand seaward. "Come to fish with my uncle, Klake Tyee. This good fishing-ground."

"It's a pretty fine country," said Ted, glancing at the scene, which bore charm to other than boyish eyes. To the east were the mountains sheltering a valley through which the frozen river wound like a silver ribbon, widening toward the sea. A cold green glacier filled the valley between two mountains with its peaks of beauty. Toward the shore, which swept in toward the river's mouth in a sheltered cove, were clumps of trees, giant fir, aspen, and hemlock, green and beautiful, while seaward swept the waves in white-capped loveliness.

Kalitan ushered them to the camp with great politeness and considerable pride.

"You've a good place to camp," said Mr. Strong, "and we will gladly share your fire until we are warm enough to go on."

Ted's face fell. "Must we go right away?" he asked. "This is such a jolly place."

"No go to-day," said Kalitan, briefly, to Chetwoof. "Colesnass."

"Huh!" said Chetwoof. "Think some."

"Here comes my uncle," said Kalitan, and he ran eagerly to meet an old Indian who came toward the camp from the shore. He eagerly explained the situation to the Tyee, who welcomed the strangers with grave politeness. He was an old man, with a seamed, scarred face, but kindly eyes. Chief of the Thlinkits, his tribe was scattered, his children dead, and Kalitan about all left to him of interest in life.

"There will be more snow," he said to Mr. Strong. "You are welcome. Stay and share our fire and food."

"Do let us stay, father," cried Ted, and his father smiled indulgently, but Kalitan looked at him in astonishment. Alaskan boys are taught to hold their tongues and let their elders decide matters, and Kalitan would never have dreamed of teasing for anything.

But Mr. Strong did not wish to face another snow-storm in the sledge, and knew he could work but little till the storm was passed; so he readily consented to stay a few days and let Ted see some real Alaskan hunting and fishing.

Both boys were delighted, and soon had the camp rearranged to accommodate the strangers. The fire was built up, Ted and Kalitan gathering cones and fir branches, which made a fragrant blaze, while Chetwoof cared for the dogs, and the old chief helped Mr. Strong pitch his tent in the lee of some fragrant firs. Soon all was prepared and supper cooking over the coals,—a supper of fresh fish and seal fat, which Alaskans consider a great delicacy, and to which Mr. Strong added coffee and crackers from his stores,—and Indians and whites ate together in friendliness and amity.

CHAPTER II

AROUND THE CAMP-FIRE

"HOW does it happen that you speak English, Kalitan?" asked Mr. Strong as they sat around the camp-fire that evening. The snow had continued during the afternoon, and the boys had had an exciting time coasting and snow-balling and enjoying themselves generally.

"I went for a few months to the Mission School at Wrangel," said Kalitan. "I learned much there. They teach the boys to read and write and do sums and to work the ground besides. They learn much more than the girls."

"Huh!" said the old chief, grimly. "Girls learn too much. They no good for Indian wives, and white men not marry them. Best for girls to stay at home at the will of their fathers until they get husbands."

"So you've been in Wrangel," said Ted to Kalitan. "We went there, too. It's a dandy place. Do you remember the fringe of white mountains back of the harbour? The people said the woods were full of game, but we didn't have time to go hunting. There are a few shops there, but it seemed to me a very small place to have been built since 1834. In the States whole towns grow up in two or three weeks."

"Huh!" said Kalitan, with a quick shrug of his shoulders, "quick grow, sun fade and wind blow down."

"I don't think the sun could ever fade in Wrangel," laughed Ted. "They told me there it hadn't shone but fifteen days in three months. It rained all the time."

"Rain is nothing," said Kalitan. "It is when the Ice Spirit speaks in the North Wind's roar and in the crackling of the floes that we tremble. The glaciers are the children of the Mountain Spirit whom our fathers worshipped. He is angry, and lo! he hurls down icebergs in his wrath, he tosses them about, upon the streams he tosses the kyaks like feathers and washes the land with the waves of Sitth. When our people are buried in the ground instead of being burnt with the fire, they must go for ever to the place of Sitth, of everlasting cold, where never sun abides, nor rain, nor warmth."

Ted had listened spellbound to this poetic speech and gazed at Kalitan in open-mouthed amazement. A boy who could talk like that was a new and delightful playmate, and he said:

"Tell me more about things, Kalitan," but the Indian was silent, ashamed of having spoken.

"What do you do all day when you are at home?" persisted the American.

"In winter there is nothing to do but to hunt and fish," said Kalitan. "Sometimes we do not find much game, then we think of how, when a Thlinkit dies, he has plenty. If he has lived as a good tribesman, his kyak glides smoothly over the silver waters into the sunset, until, o'er gently flowing currents, it reaches the place of the mighty forest. A bad warrior's canoe passes dark whirlpools and terrible rapids until he reaches the place we speak not of, where reigns Sitth.

"In the summer-time we still hunt and fish. Many have learned to till the ground, and we gather berries and wood for the winter. The other side of the inlet, the tree-trunks drift from the Yukon and are stranded on the islands, so there is plenty for firewood. But upon our island the women gather a vine and dry it. They collect seaweed for food in the early spring, and dry it and press it into square cakes, which make good food after they have hung long in the sun. They make baskets and sell them to the white people. Often my uncle and I take them to Valdez, and once we brought back fifty dollars for those my mother made. There is always much to do."

"Don't you get terribly cold hunting in the winter?" asked Ted.

"Thlinkit boy not a baby," said Kalitan, a trifle scornfully. "We begin to be hardened when we are babies. When I was five years old, I left my father and went to my uncle to be taught. Every morning I bathed in the ocean, even if I had to break ice to find water, and then I rolled in the snow. After that my uncle brushed me with a switch bundle, and not lightly, for his arm is strong. I must not cry out, no matter if he hurt, for a chief's son must never show pain nor fear. That would give his people shame."

"Don't you get sick?" asked Ted, who felt cold all over at the idea of being treated in such a heroic manner.

"The Kooshta comes sometimes," said Kalitan. "The Shaman used to cast him out, but now the white doctor can do it, unless the kooshta is too strong."

Ted was puzzled as to Kalitan's exact meaning, but did not like to ask too many questions for fear of being impolite, so he only said:

"Being sick is not very nice, anyhow."

"To be bewitched is the most terrible," said Kalitan, gravely.

"How does that happen?" asked Ted, eagerly, but Kalitan shook his head.

"It is not good to hear," he said. "The medicine-man must come with his drum and rattle, and he is very terrible. If the white men will not allow any more the punishing of the witches, they should send more of the white medicine-men, if we are not to have any more of our own."

"Boys should not talk about big things," said the old chief suddenly. He had been sitting quietly over the fire, and spoke so suddenly that Kalitan collapsed into silence. Ted, too, quieted down at the old chief's stern voice and manner, and both boys sat and listened to the men talking, while the snow still swirled about them.

Tyee Klake told Mr. Strong many interesting things about the coast country, and gave him valuable information as to the route he should pursue in his search for interesting things in the mountains.

"It will be two weeks before the snow will break so you can travel in comfort," he said. "Camp with us. We remain here one week, then we go to the island. We can take you there, you will see many things, and your boy will hunt with Kalitan."

"Where is your island?" asked Mr. Strong.

Ted said nothing, but his eyes were fixed eagerly upon his father. It was easy to see that he wished to accept the invitation.

"Out there." Tyee Klake pointed toward where the white coast-line seemed to fade into silvery blue.

"There are many islands; on some lives no one, but we have a village. Soon it will be nearly deserted, for many of our people rove during the summer, and wander from one camping-ground to another, seeking the best game or fish. But Kalitan's people remain always on the island. Him I take with me to hunt the whale and seal, to gather the berries, and to trap the little animals who bear fur. We find even seal upon our shores, though fewer since your people have come among us."

"Which were the best, Russians or Americans?" asked Mr. Strong, curious to see what the old Indian would say, but the Tyee was not to be caught napping.

"Men all alike," he said. "Thlinkit, Russian, American, some good, some bad. Russians used Indians more, gave them hunting and fishing, and only took part of the skins. Americans like to hunt and fish all themselves and leave nothing for the Indians. Russians teach quass, Americans teach whiskey. Before white men came, Indians were healthy. They ate fish, game, berries; now they must have other foods, and they are not good for Indians here,"—he touched his stomach. "Indian used to dress in skins and furs, now he must copy white man and shiver with cold. He soon has the coughing sickness and then he goes into the unknown.

"But the government of the Americans is best because it tries to do some things for the Indian. It teaches our boys useful things in the schools, and, if some of its people are bad, some Indians are bad, too. Men all alike," he repeated with the calm stoicism of his race.

"The government is far away," said Mr. Strong, "and should not be blamed for the doings of all its servants. I should like to see this island home of yours, and think we must accept your invitation; shall we, Ted?" he smiled at the boy.

"Yes, indeed; thank you, sir," said Ted, and he and Kalitan grinned at each other happily.

"We shall stay in camp until the blue jay comes," said the old chief, smiling, "and then seek the village of my people."

"What does the blue jay mean?" asked Ted, timidly, for he was very much in awe of this grave old man.

Kalitan said something in Thlinkit to his uncle, and the old chief, looking kindly at the boy, replied with a nod:

"I will tell you the story of the blue jay," he said.

"My story is of the far, far north. Beside a salmon stream there dwelt people rich in slaves. These caught and dried the salmon for the winter, and nothing is better to eat than dried salmon dipped in seal oil. All the fish were caught and stored away, when lo! the whiteness fell from heaven and the snows were upon them. It was the time of snow and they should not have complained, but the chief was evil and he cursed the whiteness. No one should dare to speak evil of the Snow Spirit, which comes from the Unknown! Deeper and deeper grew the snow. It flew like feathers about the eglu, and the slaves had many troubles in putting in limbs for the fire. Then the snow came in flakes so large they seemed like the wings of birds, and the house was covered, and they could no longer keep their kyaks on top of the snow. All were shut tight in the house, and their fire and food ran low. They knew not how many days they were shut in, for there was no way to tell the day from night, only they knew they were sore hungry and that the Snow Spirit was angry and terrible in his anger.

"But each one spoke not; he only chose a place where he should lie down and die when he could bear no more.

"Only the chief spoke, and he once. 'Snow Spirit,' he said aloud, 'I alone am evil. These are not so. Slay me and spare!' But the Snow Spirit answered not, only the wind screamed around the eglu, and his screams were terrible and sad. Then hope left the heart of the chief and he prepared to die with all his people and all his slaves.

"But on the day when their last bit of food was gone, lo! something pecked at the top of the smoke-hole, and it sang 'Nuck-tee,' and it was a blue jay. The chief heard and saw and wondered, and, looking 'neath the smoke-hole, he saw a scarlet something upon the floor.

Picking it up, he found it was a bunch of Indian tomato berries, red and ripe, and quickly hope sprang in his breast.

"'Somewhere is summer,' he cried. 'Let us up and away.'

"Then the slaves hastened to dig out the canoe, and they drew it with mighty labour, for they were weak from fasting, over the snows to the shore, and there they launched it without sail or paddle, with all the people rejoicing. And after a time the wind carried them to a beach where all was summer. Birds sang, flowers bloomed, and berries gleamed scarlet in the sun, and there were salmon jumping in the blue water. They ate and were satisfied, for it was summer on the earth and summer in their hearts.

"That is how the Thlinkits came to our island, and so we say when the snow breaks, that now comes the blue jay."

"Thank you for telling us such a dandy story," cried Ted, who had not lost a word of this quaint tale, told so graphically over the camp-fire of the old chief Klake.

CHAPTER III

TO THE GLACIER

TED slept soundly all night, wrapped in the bearskins from the sledge, in the little tent he shared with his father. When the morning broke, he sprang to his feet and hurried out of doors, hopeful for the day's pleasures. The snow had stopped, but the ground was covered with a thick white pall, and the mountains were turned to rose colour in the morning sun, which was rising in a blaze of glory.

"Good morning, Kalitan," shouted Ted to his Indian friend, whom he spied heaping wood upon the camp-fire. "Isn't it dandy? What can we do to-day?"

"Have breakfast," said Kalitan, briefly. "Then do what Tyee says."

"Well, I hope he'll say something exciting," said Ted.

"Think good day to hunt," said Kalitan, as he prepared things for the morning meal.

"Where did you get the fish?" asked Ted.

"Broke ice-hole and fished when I got up," said the Thlinkit.

"You don't mean you have been fishing already," exclaimed the lazy Ted, and Kalitan smiled as he said:

"White people like fish. Tyee said: 'Catch fish for Boston men's breakfast,' and I go."

"Do you always mind him like that?" asked Ted. He generally obeyed his father, but there were times when he wasn't anxious to and argued a little about it. Kalitan looked at him in astonishment.

"He chief!" he said, simply.

"What will we do with the camp if we all go hunting?" asked Ted.

"Nothing," said Kalitan.

"Leave Chetwoof to watch, I suppose," continued Ted.

"Watch? Why?" asked Kalitan.

"Why, everything; some one will steal our things," said Ted.

"Thlinkits not steal," said Kalitan, with dignity. "Maybe white man come along and steal from his brothers; Indians not. If we go away to long hunt, we cache blankets and no one would touch."

"What do you mean by cache?" asked Ted.

"We build a mound hut near the house, and put there the blankets and stores. Sometime they stay there for years, but no one would take from acache. If one has plenty of wood by the seashore or in the forest, he may cord it and go his way and no one will touch it. A deer hangs on a tree where dogs may not reach it, but no stray hunter would slice even a piece. We are not thieves."

"It is a pity you could not send missionaries to the States, you Thlinkits, my boy," said Mr. Strong, who had come up in time to hear Kalitan's words. "I'm afraid white people are less honest."

"Teddy, do you know we are to have some hunting to-day, and that you'll get your first experience with a glacier."

"Hurrah," shouted Ted, dancing up and down in excitement.

"Tyee Klake says we can hunt toward the base of the glacier, and I shall try to go a little ways upon it and see how the land lies, or, rather, the ice. It is getting warmer, and, if it continues a few days, the snow will melt enough to let us go over to that island you are so anxious to see."

Ted's eyes shone, and the amount of breakfast he put away quite prepared him for his day's work, which, pleasant though it might be, certainly was hard work. The chief said they must seek the glacier first before the sun got hot, for it was blinding on the snow. So they set out soon after breakfast, leaving Chetwoof in charge of the camp, and with orders to catch enough fish for dinner.

"We'll be ready to eat them, heads and tails," said Ted, and his father added, laughingly:

"'Bible, bones, and hymn-book, too.'"

"What does that mean?" asked Ted, as Kalitan looked up inquiringly.

"Once a writer named Macaulay said he could make a rhyme for any word in the English language, and a man replied, 'You can't rhyme Timbuctoo.' But he answered without a pause:

"If I were a Cassowary

On the plains of Timbuctoo,

I'd eat up a missionary,

Bible, bones, and hymn-book, too."

Ted laughed, but Kalitan said, grimly:

"Not good to eat Boston missionary, he all skin and bone!"

"Where did they get the name Alaska?" asked Ted, as they tramped over the snow toward the glacier.

"Al-ay-ck-sa—great country," said Kalitan.

"It certainly is," said Ted. "It's fine! I never saw anything like this at home," pointing as he spoke to the scene in front of him.

A group of evergreen trees, firs and the Alaska spruce, so useful for fires and torches, fringed the edge of the ice-field, green and verdant in contrast to the gleaming snows of the mountain, which rose in a gentle slope at first, then precipitously, in a dazzling and enchanting combination of colour. It was as if some marble palace of old rose before them against the heavens, for the ice was cut and serrated into spires and gables, turrets and towers, all seeming to be ornamented with fretwork where the sun's rays struck the peaks and turned them into silver and gold. Lower down the ice looked like animals, so twisted was it into fantastic shapes; fierce sea monsters with yawning mouths seeming ready to devour; bears and wolves, whales, gigantic elephants, and snowy tigers, tropic beasts looking strangely out of place in this arctic clime.

Deep crevices cut the ice-fields, and in their green-blue depths lurked death, for the least misstep would dash the traveller into an abyss which had no bottom. Beyond the glacier itself, the snow-capped mountains rose grand and serene, their glittering peaks clear against the blue sky, which hue the glacier reflected and played with in a thousand glinting shades, from purpling amethyst to lapis lazuli and turquoise.

As they gazed spellbound, a strange thing occurred, a thing of such wonder and beauty that Ted could but grasp his father's arm in silence.

Suddenly the peaks seemed to melt away, the white ice-pinnacles became real turrets, houses and cathedrals appeared, and before them arose a wonderful city of white marble, dream-like and shadowy, but beautiful as Aladdin's palace in the "Arabian Nights." At last Ted could keep silent no longer.

"What is it?" he cried, and the old chief answered, gravely:

"The City of the Dead," but his father said:

"A mirage, my boy. They are often seen in these regions, but you are fortunate in seeing one of the finest I have ever witnessed."

"What is a mirage?" demanded Ted.

"An optical delusion," said his father, "and one I am sure I couldn't explain so that you would understand it. The queer thing about a mirage is that you usually see the very thing most unlikely to be found in that particular locality. In the Sahara, men see flowers and trees and fountains, and here on this glacier we see a splendid city."

"It certainly is queer. What makes glaciers, daddy?" Ted was even more interested than usual in his father's talk because of Kalitan, whose dark eyes never left Mr. Strong's face, and who seemed to drink in every word of information as eagerly as a thirsty bird drinks water.

"The dictionaries tell you that glaciers are fields of ice, or snow and ice, formed in the regions of perpetual snow, and moving slowly down the mountain slopes or valleys. Many people say the glaciers are the fathers of the icebergs which float at sea, and that these are broken off the glacial stream, but others deny this. When the glacial ice and snow reaches a point where the air is so warm that the ice melts as fast as it is pushed down from above, the glacier ends and a river begins. These are the finest glaciers in the world, except, perhaps, those of the Himalayas.

"This bids fair to be a wonderfully interesting place for my work, Ted, and I'm glad you're likely to be satisfied with your new friends, for I shall have to go to many places and do a lot of things less interesting than the things Kalitan can show you.

"See these blocks of fine marble and those superb masses of porphyry and chalcedony,—but there's something which will interest you more. Take my gun and see if you can't bring down a bird for supper."

Wild ducks were flying low across the edge of the glacier and quite near to the boys, and Ted grasped his father's gun in wild excitement. He was never allowed to touch a gun at home. Dearly as he loved his mother, it had always seemed very strange to him that she should show such poor taste about firearms, and refuse to let him have any; and now that he had a gun really in his hands, he could hardly hold it, he was so excited. Of course it was not the first time, for his father had allowed him to practise shooting at a mark ever since they had reached Alaska, but this was the first time he had tried to shoot a living target. He selected his duck, aimed quickly, and fired. Bang! Off went the gun, and, wonder of wonders! two ducks fell instead of one.

"Well done, Ted, that duck was twins," cried his father, laughing, almost as excited as the boy himself, and they ran to pick up the birds. Kalitan smiled, too, and quietly picked up one, saying:

"This one Kalitan's," showing, as he spoke, his arrow through the bird's side, for he had discharged an arrow as Ted fired his gun.

"Too bad, Ted. I thought you were a mighty hunter, a Nimrod who killed two birds with one stone," said Mr. Strong, but Ted laughed and said:

"So I got the one I shot at, I don't care."

They had wild duck at supper that night, for Chetwoof plucked the birds and roasted them on a hot stone over the spruce logs, and Ted, tired and wet and hungry, thought he had never tasted such a delicious meal in his life.

CHAPTER IV

TED MEETS MR. BRUIN

IT seemed to Ted as if he had scarcely touched the pillow on the nights which followed before it was daylight, and he would awake to find the sun streaming in at his tent flap. He always meant to go fishing with Kalitan before breakfast, so the moment he woke up he jumped out of bed, if his pile of fragrant pine boughs covered with skins could be called a bed, and hurried through his toilet. Quick as he tried to be, however, he was never ready before Kalitan, for, when Ted appeared, the Indian boy had always had his roll in the snow and was preparing his lines.

Kalitan was perfectly fascinated with the American boy. He thought him the most wonderful specimen of a boy that he had ever seen. He knew so much that Kalitan did not, and talked so brightly that being with Ted was to the Indian like having a book without the bother of reading. There were some things about him that Kalitan could not understand, to be sure. Ted talked to his father just as if he were another boy. He even spoke to Tyee Klake on occasions when that august personage had not only not asked him a question, but was not speaking at all. From the Thlinkit point of view, this was a most remarkable performance on Ted's part, but Kalitan thought it must be all right for a "Boston boy," for even the stern old chief seemed to regard happy-go-lucky Ted with approval.

Ted, on the other hand, thought Kalitan the most remarkable boy he had ever met in all his life. He had not been much with boys. His "Lady Mother," as he always called the gentle, brown-eyed being who ruled his father and himself, had not cared to have her little Galahad mingle with the rougher city boys who thronged the streets, and had kept him with herself a great deal. Ted had loved books, and he and his little sister Judith had lived in a pleasant atmosphere of refinement, playing happily together until the boy had grown almost to dread anything common or low. His mother knew he had moral courage, and would face any issue pluckily, but his father feared he would grow up a milksop, and thought he needed hardening.

Mrs. Strong objected to the hardening process if it consisted in turning her boy loose to learn the ways of the city streets, but had consented to his going with his father, urged thereto by fears for his health, which was not of the best, and the knowledge that he had reached the "bear and Indian" age, and it was certainly a good thing for him to have his experiences first-hand.

To Ted the whole thing was perfectly delightful. When he lay down at night, he would often like to see "Mother and Ju," but he was generally so tired that he was asleep before he had time to think enough to be really homesick. During the day there was too much doing to have any thinking time, and, since he had met this boy friend, he thought of little else but him and what they were to do next. The Tyee had assured Mr. Strong that it was perfectly safe for the boys to go about together.

"Kalitan knows all the trails," he said. "He take care of white brother. Anything come, call Chetwoof."

As Mr. Strong was very anxious to penetrate the glacier under Klake's guidance, and wanted Ted to enjoy himself to the full, he left the boys to themselves, the only stipulation being that they should not go on the water without Chetwoof.

There seemed to be always something new to do. As the days grew warmer, the ice broke in the river, and the boys tramped all over the country. Ted learned to use the bow and arrow, and brought down many a bird for supper, and proud he was when he served up for his father a wild duck, shot, plucked, and cooked all by himself.

They fished in the stream by day and set lines by night. They trapped rabbits and hares in the woods, and one day even got a silver fox, a skin greatly prized by the fur traders on account of its rarity. Kalitan insisted that Ted should have it, though he could have gotten forty dollars for it from a white trader, and Ted was rejoiced at the idea of taking it home to make a set of furs for Judith.

One day Ted had a strange experience, and not a very pleasant one, which might have been very serious had it not been for Kalitan. He had noticed a queer-looking plant on the river-bank the day before, and had stopped to pick it up, when he received such a sudden and unexpected pricking as to cause him to jump back and shout for Kalitan. His hand felt as if it had been pierced by a thousand needles, and he flew to a snow-bank to rub it with snow.

"I must have gotten hold of some kind of a cactus," he said to Kalitan, who only replied:

"Huh! picked hedgehog," as he pointed to where Ted's cactus was ambling indignantly away with every quill rattling and set straight out in anger at having his morning nap disturbed. Kalitan wrapped Ted's hand in soft mud, which took the pain out, but he couldn't use it much for the next few days, and did not feel eager to hunt when his father and the Tyee started out in the morning. Kalitan remained with him, although his eyes looked wistful, for he had heard the chief talk about bear tracks having been seen the day before. Bears were quite a rarity, but sometimes an old cinnamon or even a big black bruin would venture down in search of fresh fish, which he would catch cleverly with his great paws.

Kalitan and Ted fished awhile, and then Ted wandered away a little, wondering what lay around a point of rock which he had never yet explored. Something lay there which he had by no means expected to see, and he scarcely knew what to make of it. On the river-bank, close to the edge of the stream, was a black figure, an Indian fishing, as he supposed, and he paused to watch. The fisherman was covered with fur from head to foot, and, as Ted watched him, he seemed to have no line or rod. Going nearer, the boy grew even more puzzled, and, though the man's back was toward him, he could easily see that there was something unusual about the figure. Just as he was within hailing distance and about to shout, the figure made a quick dive toward the water and sprang back again with a fish between his paws, and Ted saw that it was a huge bear. He gave a sharp cry and then stood stock-still. The creature looked around and stood gnawing his fish and staring at Ted as stupidly as the boy stared at him. Then Ted heard a halloo behind him and Kalitan's voice:

"Run for Chetwoof, quick!"

Ted obeyed as the animal started to move off. He ran toward the camp, hearing the report of Kalitan's gun as he ran. Chetwoof, hearing the noise, hurried out, and it was but a few moments before he was at Kalitan's side. To Ted it seemed like a day before he could get back and see what was happening, but he arrived on the scene in time to see Chetwoof despatch the animal.

"Hurrah!" cried Ted. "You've killed a bear," but Chetwoof only grunted crossly.

"Very bad luck!" he said, and Kalitan explained:

"Indians don't like to kill bears or ravens. Spirits in them, maybe ancestors."

Ted looked at him in great astonishment, but Kalitan explained:

"Once, long ago, a Thlinkit girl laughed at a bear track in the snow and said: 'Ugly animal must have made that track!' But a bear heard and was angry. He seized the maiden and bore her to his den, and turned her into a bear, and she dwelt with him, until one day her brother killed the bear and she was freed. And from that day Thlinkits speak respectfully of bears, and do not try to kill them, for they know not whether it is a bear or a friend who hides within the shaggy skin."

The Tyee and Mr. Strong were greatly surprised when they came home to see the huge carcass of Mr. Bruin, and they listened to the account of Kalitan's bravery. The old chief said little, but he looked approvingly at Kalitan, and said "Hyas kloshe" (very good), which unwonted praise made the boy's face glow with pleasure. They had a great discussion as to whom the bear really belonged. Ted had found him, Kalitan had shot him first, and Chetwoof had killed him, so they decided to go shares. Ted wanted the skin to take home, and thought it would make a splendid rug for his mother's library, so his father paid Kalitan and Chetwoof what each would have received as their share had the skin been sold to a trader, and they all had bear meat for supper. Ted thought it finer than any beefsteak he had ever eaten, and over it Kalitan smacked his lips audibly.

CHAPTER V

A MONSTER OF THE DEEP

THE big bear occupied considerable attention for several days. He had to be carefully skinned and part of the meat dried for future use. Alaskans never use salt for preserving meat. Indeed they seem to dislike salt very much. It had taken Ted some time to learn to eat all his meat and fish quite fresh, without a taste of salt, but he had grown to like it. There is something in the sun and wind of Alaska which cures meat perfectly, and the bear's meat was strung on sticks and dried in the sun so that they might enjoy it for a long time.

It seemed as if the adventure with Bruin was enough to last the boys for several days, for Ted's hand still pained him from the porcupine's quills, and he felt tired and lazy. He lay by the camp-fire one afternoon listening to Kalitan's tales of his island home, when his father came in from a long tramp, and, looking at him a little anxiously, asked:

"What's the matter, son?"

"Nothing, I'm only tired," said Ted, but Kalitan said:

"Porcupine quills poison hand. Well in a few days."

"So your live cactus is getting in his work, is he? I'm glad it wasn't the bear you mistook for an Alaskan posy and tried to pick. I'm tired myself," and Mr. Strong threw himself down to rest.

"Daddy, how did we come to have Alaska, anyway?"

"Well, that's a long story," said his father, "but an interesting one."

"Do tell us about it," urged Ted. "I know we bought it, but what did we pay the Indians for it? I shouldn't have thought they'd have sold such a fine country."

Kalitan looked up quickly, and there was a sudden gleam in his dark eyes that Ted had never seen before.

"Thlinkits never sell," he said. "Russians steal."

Mr. Strong put his hand kindly on the boy's head.

"You're right, Kalitan," he said. "The Russians never conquered the Thlinkits, the bravest tribe in all Alaska.

"You see, Teddy, it was this way. A great many years ago, about 1740, a Danish sailor named Bering, who was in the service of the Russians, sailed across the ocean and discovered the strait named for him, and a number of islands. Some of these were not inhabited, others had Indians or Esquimos on them, but, after the manner of the early discoverers, Bering took possession of them all in the name of the Emperor of Russia. It doesn't seem right as we look at things now, but in those days 'might made right,' and it was just the same way the English did when they came to America.

"The Russians settled here, finding the fishing and furs fine things for trade, and driving the Indians, who would not yield to them, farther and farther inland. In 1790 the Czar made Alexander Baranoff manager of the trading company. Baranoff established trading-posts in various places, and settled at Sitka, where you can see the ruins of the splendid castle he built. The Russians also sent missionaries to convert the Indians to the Greek Church, which is the church of Russia. The Indians, however, never learned to care for the Russians, and often were cruelly treated by them. The Russians, however, tried to do something for their education, and established several schools. One as early as 1775, on Kadiak Island, had thirty

17

pupils, who studied arithmetic, reading, navigation, and four of the mechanical trades, and this is a better record than the American purchasers can show, I am sorry to say.

"One of the recent travellers in Alaska says that he met in the country 'American citizens who never in their lives heard a prayer for the President of the United States, nor of the Fourth of July, nor the name of the capital of the nation, but who have been taught to pray for the Emperor of Russia, to celebrate his birthday, and to commemorate the victories of ancient Greece.' In March, 1867, the Russians sold Alaska to the United States for $7,200,000 in gold. It was bought for a song almost, when we consider the immense amount of money made for the government by the seal fisheries, the cod and salmon industries, and the opening of the gold fields. The resources of the country are not half-known, and the government is beginning to see this. That is one of the reasons they have sent me here, with the other men, to find out what the earth holds for those who do not know how to look for its treasures. Gold is not the best thing the earth produces. There is land in Alaska little known full of coal and other useful minerals. Other land is covered with magnificent timber which could be shipped to all parts of the world. There are pasture-lands where stock will fatten like pigs without any other feeding; there are fertile soils which will raise almost any crops, and there are intelligent Indians who can be taught to work and be useful members of society. I do not mean dragged off to the United States to learn things they could never use in their home lives, but who should be educated here to make the best of their talents in their home surroundings.

"That is one crying shame to our government, that they have neglected the Alaskan citizens. Forty years have been wasted, but we are beginning to wake up now, and twenty years more will see the Indians of Kalitan's generation industrious men and women, not only clever hunters and fishermen, but lumbermen, coopers, furniture makers, farmers, miners, and stock-raisers."

At this moment their quiet conversation was interrupted by a wild shout from the shore, and, springing to their feet, they saw Chetwoof gesticulating wildly and shouting to the Tyee, who had been mending his canoe by the river-bank. Kalitan dropped everything and ran without a word, scudding like the arrow from which he took his name. Before Ted could follow or ask what was the matter, from the ocean a huge body rose ten feet out of the water, spouting jets of spray twenty feet into the air, the sun striking his sides and turning them to glistening silver. Then it fell back, the waters churning into frothy foam for a mile around.

"It's a whale, Ted, sure as you live. Luck certainly is coming your way," said his father; but, at the word "whale," Ted had started after Kalitan, losing no time in getting to the scene of action as fast as possible.

"Watch the Tyee!" called Kalitan over his shoulder, as both boys ran down to the water's edge.

The old chief was launching his kiak into the seething waters, and to Ted it seemed incredible that he meant to go in that frail bark in pursuit of the mighty monster. The old man's face, however, was as calm as though starting on a pleasure-trip in peaceful waters, and Ted watched in breathless admiration to see what would happen next.

Klake paddled swiftly out to sea, drawing as near as he dared to where the huge monster splashed idly up and down like a great puppy at play. He stopped the kiak and watched; then poised his spear and threw it, and so swift and graceful was his gesture that Ted exclaimed in amazement.

"Tyee Klake best harpoon-thrower of all the Thlinkits," said Kalitan, proudly. "Watch!"

Ted needed no such instructions. His keen eyes passed from fish to man and back again, and no movement of the Tyee escaped him.

The instant the harpoon was thrown, the Tyee paddled furiously away, for when a harpoon strikes a whale, he is likely to lash violently with his tail, and may destroy his enemy, and this is a moment of terrible danger to the harpooner. But the whale was too much astonished to fight, and, with a terrific splash, he dived deep, deep into the water, to get rid of that stinging thing in his side, in the cold green waters below.

"AWAY WENT ANOTHER STINGING LANCE."

The Tyee waited, his grim face tense and earnest. It might have been fifteen minutes, for whales often stay under water for twenty minutes before coming to the surface to breathe, but to Kalitan and Ted it seemed an hour.

Then the spray dashed high into the air again, and the instant the huge body appeared, Klake drew near, and away went another stinging lance again, swift and, oh! so sure of aim. This time the whale struck out wildly, and Kalitan held his breath, while Ted gasped at the Tyee's danger, for his kiak rocked like a shell and then was quite hidden from their sight by the spray which was dashed heavenward like clouds of white smoke.

Once more the creature dived, and this time he stayed down only a few minutes, and, when he came up, blood spouted into the air and dyed the sea crimson, and Kalitan exclaimed:

"Pierced his lungs! Now he must die."

There was one more bright, glancing weapon flying through the air, and Ted noticed attached to it by a thong a curious-looking bulb, and asked Kalitan:

"What is on that lance?"

"Sealskin buoy," said Kalitan. "We make the bag and blow it up, tie it to the harpoon, and when the lance sticks into the whale, the buoy makes it very hard for him to dive. After awhile he dies and drifts ashore."

The waters about the whale were growing red, and the carcass seemed drifting out to sea, and at last the Tyee seemed satisfied. He sent a last look toward the huge body, then turned his kiak toward the watchers on the banks.

"If it only comes to shore," said Kalitan.

"What will you do with it?" asked Ted.

"Oh, there are lots of things we can do with a whale," said Kalitan. "The blubber is the best thing to eat in all the world. Then we use the oil in a bowl with a bit of pith in it to light our huts. The bones are all useful in building our houses. Whales were once bears, but they played too much on the shore and ran away to sea, so they wore off all their fur on the rocks, and had their feet nibbled off by the fishes."

"Well, this one didn't have his tail nibbled off at any rate," laughed Ted. "I saw it flap at the Tyee, and thought that was the last of him, sure."

"Tyee much big chief," said Kalitan, and just then the old man's kiak drew near them, and he stepped ashore as calmly as though he had not just been through so exciting a scene with a mighty monster of the deep.

CHAPTER VI

THE ISLAND HOME OF KALITAN

SWIFT and even were the strokes of the paddles as the canoes sped over the water toward Kalitan's island home. Ted was so excited that he could hardly sit still, and Tyee Klake gave him a warning glance and a muttered "Kooletchika."

The day before a big canoe had come to the camp, the paddlers bearing messages for the Tyee, and he had had a long conversation with Mr. Strong. The result was astonishing to Teddy, for his father told him that he was to go for a month to the island with Kalitan. This delighted him greatly, but he was a little frightened when he found that his father was to stay behind.

"It's just this way, son," Mr. Strong explained to him. "I'm here in government employ, taking government pay to do government work. I must do it and do it well in the shortest time possible. You will have a far better time on the island with Kalitan than you could possibly have loafing around the camp here. You couldn't go to many places where I am going, and, if my mind is easy about you, I can take Chetwoof and do my work in half the time. I'll come to the island in three or four weeks, and we'll take a week's vacation together, and then we'll hit the trail for the gold-fields. Are you satisfied with this arrangement?"

"Yes, sir." Ted's tone was dubious, but his face soon cleared up. "A month won't be very long, father."

"No, I'll wager you'll be sorry to leave when I come for you. Try and not make any trouble. Of course Indian ways are not ours, but you'll get used to it all and enjoy it. It's a chance most boys would be crazy over, and you'll have tales to tell when you get home to make your playmates envy you. I'm glad I have a son I can trust to keep straight when he is out of my sight," and he laid his hand affectionately on the boy's shoulder. Ted looked his father squarely in the eye, but gave only a little nod in answer, then he laughed his clear, ringing laugh.

"Wouldn't mother have spasms!" he exclaimed. Mr. Strong laughed too, but said:

"You'll be just as well off tumbling around with Kalitan as falling off a glacier or two, as you would be certain to do if you were with me."

Teddy felt a little blue when he said good-bye to his father, but Kalitan quickly dispelled his gloom by a great piece of news.

"Great time on island," he said, as the canoe glided toward the dim outline of land to which Ted's thoughts had so often turned. "Tyee's whale came ashore. We go to see him cut up."

"Hurrah!" cried Ted, delighted. "To think I shall see all that! What else will we do, Kalitan?"

"Hunt, fish, hear old Kala-kash stories. See berry dance if you stay long enough, perhaps a potlatch; do many things," said the Indian.

One of the Indian paddlers said something to Kalitan, and he laughed a little, and Ted asked, curiously: "What did he say?"

"Said Kalitan Tenas learned to talk as much as a Boston boy," said Kalitan, laughing heartily, and Ted laughed, too.

The canoes were nearing the shore of a wooded island, and Ted saw a fringe of trees and some native houses clustered picturesquely against them at the crest of a small hill which sloped down to the water's edge, where stood a group of people awaiting the canoes.

"My home," said Kalitan, pointing to the largest house, "my people." There was a great deal of pride in his tone and look, and he received a warm welcome as the canoes touched land and their occupants sprang on shore. The boys crowded around the young Indian and chattered and gesticulated toward Ted, while a bright-looking little Malamute sprang upon Kalitan and nearly knocked him down, covering his face with eager puppy kisses.

The girls were less boisterous, and regarded Teddy with shy curiosity. Some of them were quite pretty, and the babies were as cunning as the puppies. They barked every time the dogs did, in a funny, hoarse little way, and, indeed, Alaskan babies learn to bark long before they learn to talk.

The Tyee's wife received Teddy kindly, and he soon found himself quite at home among these hospitable people, who seemed always friendly and natural. Nearly all spoke some English, and he rapidly added to his store of Chinook, so that he had no trouble in making himself understood or in understanding. Of course he missed his father, but he had little time to be lonely. Life in the village was anything but uneventful.

At first there was the whale to be attended to, and all the village turned out for that. The huge creature had drifted ashore on the farther side of the island, and Ted was much interested in seeing him gradually disposed of. Great masses of blubber were stripped from the sides to be used later both for food and fuel, the whalebone was carefully secured to be sold to the traders, and it seemed to Ted that there was not one thing in that vast carcass for which the Indians did not have some use.

Ted soon tired of watching the many things done with the whale, but there was plenty to do and see in the village.

The village houses were all alike. There was one large room in which the people cooked, ate, and slept. The girls had blankets strung across one corner, behind which were their beds. Teddy was given one also for his corner of the great room in the Tyee's house.

He learned to eat the food and to like it very much. There was dried fish, herons' eggs, berries, or those put up in seal oil, which is obtained by frying the fat out of the blubber of the seal. The Alaskans use this oil in nearly all their cooking, and are very fond of it. Ted ate also dried seaweed, chopped and boiled in seal oil, which tasted very much like boiled and salted leather, but he liked it very well. Indeed he grew so strong and well, out-of-doors all day in the clear air and bright sunshine of the Alaskan June, that he could eat anything and tramp all day without being too tired to sleep like a top all night, and wake ready for a new day with a zest he never felt at home.

Fresh fish were plentiful. The boys caught salmon, smelts, and whitefish, and many were dried for the coming winter, while clams, gum-boots, sea-cucumbers, and devil-fish, found on the rocks of the shore, were every-day diet.

Kalitan's sister and Ted became great friends. She was older than Kalitan, and, though only fifteen, was soon to be married to Tah-ge-ah, a fine young Indian who was ready to pay high for her, which was not strange, for she was both pretty and sweet.

"At the next full moon," said Kalitan, "there will be a potlatch, and Tanana will be sold to Tah-ge-ah. He says he will give four hundred blankets for her, and my uncle is well pleased. Many only pay ten blankets for a wife, but of course we would not sell my sister for that. She is of high caste, chief's daughter, niece, and sister," the boy spoke proudly, and Ted answered:

"She's so pretty, too. She's not like the Indian girls I saw at Wrangel and Juneau. Why, there the women sat around as dirty as dogs on the sidewalk, and didn't seem to care how they looked. They had baskets to sell, and were too lazy to care whether any one bought them or not. They weren't a bit like Tanana. She's as pretty as a Japanese."

Kalitan smiled, well pleased, and Ted added, "I guess the Thlinkits must be the best Indians in Alaska."

Kalitan laughed outright at this.

"Thlinkits pretty good," he said. "Tanana good girl. She learned much good at the mission school, marry Tah-ge-ah, and make people better. She can weave blankets, make fine baskets, and keep house like a white girl."

"She's all right," said Ted. "But, Kalitan, what is a potlatch?"

"Potlatch is a good-will feast," said his friend. "Very fine thing, but white men do not like. Say Indian feasts are all bad. Why is it bad when an Indian gives away all his goods for others? That is what a great potlatch is. When white men give us whiskey and it is drunk too much, then it is very bad. But Tyee will not have that for Tanana's feast. We will drink only quass, as my people made it before they learned evil drinks and fire-water, which make them crazy."

"I guess Tyee Klake was right when he said all men were alike," said Ted, sagely. "It seems to me that there are good and bad ones in all countries. It's a pity you have had such bad white ones here in Alaska, but I guess you have had good ones, too."

"Plenty good, plenty bad, Thlinkit men and Boston men," said Kalitan, "all same."

CHAPTER VII

TWILIGHT TALES AND TOTEMS

"ONCE a small girl child went by night to bring water. In the skies above she saw the Moon shining brightly, pale and placid, and she put forth her tongue at it, which was an evil thing, for the Moon is old, and a Thlinkit child should show respect for age. So the Moon would not endure so rude a thing from a girl child, and it came down from the sky and took her thither. She cried out in fear and caught at the long grass to keep herself from going up, but the Moon was strong and took her with her water-bucket and her bunch of grass, and she never came back. Her mother wept for her, but her father said: 'Cease. We have other girl children; she is now wedded to the Moon; to him we need not give a potlatch.'

"You may see her still, if you will look at the Moon, there, grass in one hand, bucket in the other, and when the new Moon tips to one side and the water spills from the clouds and it is the months of rain, it is the bad Moon maiden tipping over her water-bucket upon the earth. No Thlinkit child would dare ever to put her tongue forth at the Moon, for fear of a like fate to that of Squi-ance, the Moon maiden."

Tanana's voice was soft and low, and she looked very pretty as she sat in the moonlight at the door of the hut and told Kalitan and Ted quaint old stories. Ted was delighted with her tales, and begged for another and yet another, and Tanana told the quaint story of Kagamil.

"A mighty toyon dwelt on the island of Kagamil. By name he was Kat-haya-koochat, and he was of great strength and much to be feared. He had long had a death feud with people of the next totem, but the bold warrior Yakaga, chieftain of the tribe, married the toyon's daughter, and there was no more feud. Zampa was the son of Kat-haya-koochat, and his pride. He built for this son a fine bidarka, and the boy launched it on the sea. His father watched him sail and called him to return, lest evil befall. But Zampa heard not his father's voice and pursued diving birds, and, lo! he was far from land and the dark fell. He sailed to the nearest shore and beheld the village of Yakaga, where the people of his sister's husband made him welcome, though Yakaga was not within his hut. There was feasting and merry-making, and, according to their custom, he, the stranger, was given a chieftain's daughter to wife, and her name was Kitt-a-youx; and Zampa loved her and she him, and he returned not home. But Kitt-a-youx's father liked him not, and treated him with rudeness because of the old enmity with his Tyee father, so Zampa said to Kitt-a-youx: 'Let us go hence. We cannot be happy here. Let us go from your father, who is unfriendly to me, and seek the barrabora of my father, the mighty chief, that happiness may come upon us,' and Kitt-a-youx said: 'What my lord says is well.'

"Then Zampa placed her in his canoe, and alone beneath the stars they sailed and it was well, and Zampa's arm was strong at his paddle. But, lo! they heard another paddle, and one came after them, and soon arrows flew about them, arrows swift and cruel, and one struck his paddle from his hand and his canoe was overturned. The pursuer came and placed Kitt-a-youx in his canoe, seeking, too, for Zampa, but, alas! Zampa was drowned. And when his pursuer dragged his body to the surface, he gave a mighty cry, for, lo! it was his brother-in-law whom he had pursued, for he was Yakaga. Then fearing the terrible rage of Zampa's father, he dared not return with the body, so he left it with the overturned canoe in the kelp and weeds. Kitt-a-youx he bore with him to his own island. There she was sad as the sea-gull's scream, for the lord she loved was dead. And her father gave her to another toyon, who was cruel to her, and her life was as a slave's, and she loathed her life until Zampa's child was born to her, and for it she lived. Alas, it was a girl child and her husband hated it, and Kitt-a-youx saw nothing for it but to be sold as a slave as was she herself. And she looked by day and by night at the sea, and its cold, cold waves seemed warmer to her than the arms of men.

'With my girl child I shall go hence,' she whispered to herself, 'and the Great Unknown Spirit will be kind.'

"So by night she stole away in a canoe and steered to sea, ere she knew where she was, reaching the seaweeds where she had journeyed with her young husband. The morning broke, and she saw the weeds and the kelp where her lover had gone from her sight, and, with a glad sigh, she clasped Zampa's child to her breast and sank down among the weeds where he had died. So her tired spirit was at rest, for a woman is happier who dies with him she loves.

"Now Zampa's father had found his boy's body and mourned over it, and buried it in a mighty cave, the which he had once made for his furs and stores. With it he placed bows and arrows and many valuables in respect for the dead. And Zampa's sister, going to his funeral feast, fell upon a stone with her child, so that both were killed. Then broke the old chief's heart. Beside her brother he laid her in the cave, and gave orders that he himselfshould be placed there as well, when grief should have made way with him. Then he died of sorrow for his children, and his people interred him in his burial cave, and with him they put much wealth and blankets and weapons.

"When, therefore, the people of his tribe found the bodies of Kitt-a-youx and her child among the kelp, having heard of her love for Zampa, they bore them to the same cave, and, wrapping them in furs, they placed Kitt-a-youx beside her beloved husband, and in her burial she found her home and felt the kindness of the Great Spirit. This, then, is the story of the burial cave of Kagamil, and since that day no man dwelt upon the island, and it is known as the 'island of the dead.'"

"I'd like to see it, I can tell you," said Ted. "Are there any burial caves around here?"

"The Thlinkits do not bury in caves," said Tanana. "We used to burn our dead, but often we place them in totem-poles."

"I thought those great poles by your doors were totems," said Ted, puzzled.

"Yes," said the girl. "They are caste totems, and all who are of any rank have them. As we belong to the Raven, or Bear, or Eagle clan, we have the carved poles to show our rank, but the totem of the dead is quite different. It does not stand beside the door, but far away. It is alone, as the soul of the dead in whose honour it is made. It is but little carved. A square hole is cut at the back of the pole, and the body of the dead, wrapped in a matting of cedar bark, is placed within, a board being nailed so that the body will not fall to the ground. A potlatch is given, and food from the feast is put in the fire for the dead person."

"It seems queer to put weapons and blankets and things to eat on people's graves," said Ted. "Why do they do it?"

"Of the dead we know nothing," said Tanana. "Perhaps the warrior spirit wishes his arrows in the Land of the Great Unknown."

"Yes, but he can't come back for them," persisted Ted.

"At Wrangel, Boston man put flowers on his girl's grave," said Kalitan, drily. "She come back and smell posy?"

Having no answer ready, Ted changed the subject and asked:

"Why do you have the raven at the top of your totem pole?"

"Indian cannot marry same totem," said Kalitan. "My father was eagle totem, my mother was raven totem. He carve her totem at the top of the pole, then his totem and those of the family are carved below. The greater the family the taller the totem."

"How do you get these totems?" demanded Ted.

"Clan totems we take from our parents, but a man may choose his own totem. Before he becomes a man he must go alone into the forest to fast, and there he chooses his totem, and he is brother to that animal all his life, and may not kill it. When he comes forth, he may take part in all the ceremonies of his tribe."

"Why, it is something like knighthood and the vigil at arms and escutcheons, and all those Round-Table things," exclaimed Ted, in delight, for he dearly loved the stirring tales of King Arthur and his knights and the doughty deeds of Camelot.

"Tell us about that," said Kalitan, so Ted told them many tales in the moonlight, as they sat beneath the shadows of the quaint and curious totem-poles of Kalitan's tribe.

CHAPTER VIII

THE BERRY DANCE

TEDDY'S month upon the island stretched out into two. His father came and went, finding the boy so happy and well that he left him with an easy mind. Ted's fair skin was tanned to a warm brown, and, clad in Indian clothes, save for his aureole of copper-coloured hair, so strong a contrast to the straight black locks of his Indian brothers, he could hardly be told from one of the island lads who roamed all day by wood and shore. They called him "Yakso pil chicamin," and all the village liked him.

Tanana's marriage-feast was held, and she and Tah-ge-ah went to housekeeping in a little hut, where the one room was as clean and neat as could be, and not a bit like the dirty rooms of some of the natives. Tanana spent all her spare time weaving beautiful baskets, for her slim fingers were very skilful. Some of the baskets which she made out of the inner bark of the willow-tree were woven so closely that they would hold water, and Teddy never tired of watching her weave the gay colours in and out, nor of seeing the wonderful patterns grow. Tah-ge-ah would take them to the mainland when she had enough made, and sell them to the travellers from the States. Meantime Tah-ge-ah himself was very, very busy carving the totem-pole for his new home, for Tanana was a chieftain's daughter, and he, too, was of high caste, and their totem must be carved and stand one hundred feet high beside their door, lest they be reproached.

Ted also enjoyed seeing old Kala-kash carve, for he was the finest carver among the Indians, and it was wonderful to see him cut strange figures out of bone, wood, horn, fish-bones, and anything his gnarled old fingers could get hold of, and he would carve grasshoppers, bears, minnows, whales, sea-gulls, babies, or idols. He made, too, a canoe for Ted, a real Alaskan dugout, shaping the shell from a log and making it soft by steam, filling the hole with water and throwing in red-hot stones. The wood was then left to season, and Ted could hardly wait patiently until sun and wind and rain had made his precious craft seaworthy. Then it was painted with paint made by rubbing a certain rock over the surface of a coarse stone and the powder mixed with oil or water.

At last it was done, a shapely thing, more beautiful in Ted's eyes than any launch or yacht he had ever seen at home. His canoe had a carved stern and a sharp prow which came out of the water, and which had carved upon it a fine eagle. Kala-kash had not asked Ted what his totem was, but supposing that the American eagle on the buttons of the boy's coat was his emblem, had carved the rampant bird upon the canoe as the boy's totem. Ted learned to paddle and to fish, never so well as Kalitan, of course, for he was born to it, but still he did very well, and enjoyed it hugely.

Happily waned the summer days, and then came the time of the berry dance, which Kalitan had spoken of so often that Ted was very anxious to see it.

The salmon-berry was fully ripe, a large and luscious berry, found in two colours, yellow and dark red. Besides these there were other small berries, maruskins, like the New England dewberries, huckleberries, and whortleberries.

"We have five kinds of berries on our island," said Kalitan. "All good. The birds, flying from the mainland, first brought the seeds, and our berries grow larger than almost any place in Alaska."

"They're certainly good," said Ted, his mouth full as he spoke. "These salmon-berries are a kind of a half-way between our blackberries and strawberries. I never saw anything prettier than the way the red and yellow berries grow so thick on the same bush—"

"There come the canoes!" interrupted Kalitan, and the two boys ran down to the water's edge, eager to be the first to greet the visitors. Tyee Klake was giving a feast to the people of the neighbouring islands, and a dozen canoes glided over the water from different directions. The canoes were all gaily decorated, and they came swiftly onward to the weird chant of the paddlers, which the breeze wafted to the listeners' ears in a monotonous melody.

Every one in the village had been astir since daybreak, preparing for the great event. Parallel lines had been strung from the chief's house to the shore, and from these were hung gay blankets, pieces of bright calico, and festoons of leaves and flowers. As the canoes landed their occupants, the dancers thronged to welcome their guests. The great drum sounded its loud note, and the dancers, arrayed in wonderful blankets woven in all manner of fanciful designs and trimmed with long woollen fringes, swayed back and forth, up and down, to and fro, in a very graceful manner, keeping time to the music.

In the centre of the largest canoe stood the Tyee of a neighbouring island, a tall Indian, dressed in a superb blanket with fringe a foot long, fringed leggins and moccasins of walrus hide, and the chief's hat to show his rank. It was a peculiar head-dress half a foot high, trimmed in down and feathers.

The Tyee, in perfect time to the music, swayed back and forth, never ceasing for a moment, shaking his head so that the down was wafted in a snowy cloud all over him.

As the canoes reached the shallows, the shore Indians dashed into the water to draw them up to land, and the company was joyously received. Teddy was delighted, for in one of the canoes was his father, whom he had not seen for several weeks. After the greetings were over, the dancers arranged themselves in opposite lines, men on one side, women on the other, and swayed their bodies while the drum kept up its unceasing tum-tum-tum.

"It's a little bit like square dances at home," said Ted. "It's ever so pretty, isn't it? First they sway to the right, then to the left, over and over and over; then they bend their bodies forward and backward without bending their knees, then sway again, and bend to one side and then the other, singing all the time. Isn't it odd, father?"

"It certainly is, but it's very graceful," said Mr. Strong. "Some of the girls are quite pretty, gentle-looking creatures, but the older women are ugly."

"The very old women look like the mummies in the museum at home," said Ted. "There's one old woman, over a hundred years old, whose skin is like a piece of parchment, and she wears the hideous lip-button which most of the Thlinkits have stopped using. Kalitan says all the women used to wear them. The girls used to make a cut in their chins between the lip and the chin, and put in a piece of wood, changing it every few days for a piece a little larger until the opening was stretched like a second mouth. When they grew up, a wooden button like the bowl of a spoon was set in the hole and constantly enlarged. The largest I have seen was three inches long. Isn't it a curious idea, father?"

"It certainly is, but there is no telling what women will admire. A Chinese lady binds her feet, and an American her waist; a Maori woman slits her nose, and an English belle pierces her ears. It's on the same principle that your Thlinkit friends slit their chins for the lip-button."

"I'm mighty glad they don't do it now, for Tanana's as pretty as a pink, and it would be a shame to spoil her face that way," said Ted. "The dancing has stopped, father; let's see what they'll do next. There comes Kalitan."

A feast of berries was to follow the dance, and Kalitan led Mr. Strong and Ted to the chief's house, which was gaily decorated with blankets and bits of bright cloth. A table covered with a cloth was laid around three sides of the room, and on this was spread hardtack and huge bowls of berries of different colours. These were beaten up with sugar into a foamy mixture, pink, purple, and yellow, according to the colour of the berries, which tasted good and looked pretty.

Ted and Kalitan had helped gather the berries, and their appetites were quite of the best. Mr. Strong smiled to see how the once fussy little gentleman helped himself with a right good-will to the Indian dainties of his friends.

Many pieces of goods had been provided for the potlatch, and these were given away, given and received with dignified politeness. There was laughing and merriment with the feast, and when it was all over, the canoes floated away as they had come, into the sunset, which gilded all the sea to rosy, golden beauty.

Ted's share of the potlatch was a beautiful blanket of Tanana's weaving, and he was delighted beyond measure.

"You're a lucky boy, Ted," said his father. "People pay as high as sixty-five dollars for an Alaskan blanket, and not always a perfect one at that. Many of the Indians are using dyed yarns to weave them, but yours is the genuine article, made from white goat's wool, long and soft, and dyed only in the native reds and blacks. We shall have to do something nice for Tanana when you leave."

"I'd like to give her something, and Kalitan, too." Ted's face looked very grave. "When do I have to go, father?"

"Right away, I'm afraid," was the reply. "I've let you stay as long as possible, and now we must start for our northern trip, if you are to see anything at all of mines and Esquimos before we start home. The mail-steamer passes Nuchek day after to-morrow, and we must go over there in time to take it."

"Yes, sir," said Ted, forlornly. He wanted to see the mines and all the wonderful things of the far north, but he hated to leave his Indian friends.

"What's the trouble, Ted?" His father laid his hand on his shoulder, disliking to see the bright face so clouded.

"I was only thinking of Kalitan," said Ted.

"Suppose we take Kalitan with us," said Mr. Strong.

"Oh, daddy, could we really?" Ted jumped in excitement.

"I'll ask the Tyee if he will lend him to us for a month," said Mr. Strong, and in a few minutes it was decided, and Ted, with one great bear's hug to thank his father, rushed off to find his friend and tell him the glorious news.

CHAPTER IX

ON THE WAY TO NOME

"WELL, boys, we're off for a long sail, and I'm afraid you will be rather tired with the steamer before you are done with her," said Mr. Strong. They had boarded the mail-steamer late the night before, and, going right to bed, had wakened early next day and rushed on deck to find the August sun shining in brilliant beauty, the islands quite out of sight, and nought but sea and sky around and above them.

"Oh, I don't know; we'll find something to do," said Teddy. "You'll have to tell us lots about the places we pass, and, if there aren't any other boys on board, Kalitan and I will be together. What's the first place we stop?"

"We passed the Kenai Peninsula in the night. I wish you could have caught a glimpse of some of the waterfalls, volcanoes, and glaciers. They are as fine as any in Alaska," said Mr. Strong. "Our next stop will be Kadiak Island."

"Kadiak Island was once near the mainland," said Kalitan. "There was only the narrowest passage of water, but a great Kenai otter tried to swim the pass, and was caught fast. He struggled so that he made it wider and wider, and at last pushed Kadiak way out to sea."

"He must have been a whopper," said Ted, "to push it so far away. Is that the island?"

"Yes," said his father. "There are no splendid forests on the island as there are on the mainland, but the grasses are superb, for the fog and rain here keeps them green as emerald."

"What a queer canoe that Indian has!" exclaimed Ted. "It isn't a bit like yours, Kalitan."

"It is bidarka," said Kalitan. "Kadiak people make canoe out of walrus hide. They stretch it over frames of driftwood. It holds two people. They sit in small hatch with apron all around their bodies, and the bidarka goes over the roughest sea and floats like a bladder. Big bidarka called anoomiak, and holds whole family."

"Some one has called the bidarkas the 'Cossacks of the sea,'" said Mr. Strong. "They skim along like swallows, and are as perfectly built as any vessel I ever saw."

"What are those huge buildings on the small island?" asked Ted, as the steamer wound through the shallows.

"Ice-houses," said his father. "Before people learned to manufacture ice, immense cargoes were shipped from here to as far south as San Francisco."

"It was fun to see them go fishing for ice from the steamer when we came up to Skaguay," said Ted. "The sailors went out in a boat, slipped a net around a block of ice and towed it to the side of the ship, then it was hitched to a derrick and swung on deck."

"Huh!" said Kalitan. "What people want ice for stored up? Think they'd store sunshine!"

"If you could invent a way to do that, you could make a fortune, my boy," said Mr. Strong, laughing. "The next place of any interest is Karluk. It's around on the other side of the island in Shelikoff Strait, and is famous for its salmon canneries. Nearly half of the entire salmon pack of Alaska comes from Kadiak Island, most of the fish coming from the Karluk River."

"Very bad for Indians," said Kalitan. "Used to have plenty fish. Tyee Klake said salmon used to come up this river in shoal sixteen miles long, and now Boston men take them all."

"It does seem a pity that the Indians don't even have a chance to earn their living in the canneries," said Mr. Strong. "The largest cannery in the world is at Karluk. There are thousands of men employed, and in one year over three million salmon were packed, yet with all this work for busy hands to do, the canneries employ Chinese, Greek, Portuguese, and American workmen in preference to the Indians, bringing them by the shipload from San Francisco."

"What other places do we pass?" asked Ted.

"A lot of very interesting ones, and I wish we could coast along, stopping wherever we felt like it," said Mr. Strong. "The Shumagin Islands are where Bering, the great discoverer and explorer, landed in 1741 to bury one of his crew. Codfish were found there, and Captain Cook, in his 'Voyages and Discoveries,' speaks of the same fish. There is a famous fishery there now called the Davidson Banks, and the codfishing fleet has its headquarters on Popoff Island. Millions of codfish are caught here every year. These islands are also a favourite haunt of the sea otter. Belofsky, at the foot of Mt. Pavloff, is the centre of the trade."

MOUNT SHISHALDIN.

"What kind of fur is otter?" asked Ted, whose mind was so inquiring that his father often called him the "living catechism."

"It is the court fur of China and Russia, and at one time the common people were forbidden by law to wear it," said Mr. Strong. "It is a rich, purplish brown sprinkled with silver-tipped hairs, and the skins are very costly."

"At one time any one could have otter," said Kalitan. "We hunted them with spears and bows and arrows. Now they are very few, and we find them only in dangerous spots, hiding on rocks or floating kelp. Sometimes the hunters have to lie in hiding for days watching them. Only Indians can kill the otter. Boston men can if they marry Indian women. That makes them Indian."

"Rather puts otter at a discount and women at a premium," laughed Mr. Strong. "Now we pass along near the Alaska peninsula, past countless isles and islets, through the Fox Islands to Unalaska, and then into the Bering Sea. One of the most interesting things in this region is called the 'Pacific Ring of Fire,' a chain of volcanoes which stretches along the coast. Often the passengers can see from the ships at night a strange red glow over the sky, and know that the fire mountains are burning. The most beautiful of these volcanoes is Mt. Shishaldin, nearly nine thousand feet high, and almost as perfect a cone in shape as Fuji Yama, which the Japanese love so much and call 'the Honourable Mountain.' At Unalaska or Ilinlink, the 'curving beach,' we stop. If we could stay over for awhile, there are a great many interesting things we could see; an old Greek church and the government school are in the town, and Bogoslov's volcano and the sea-lion rookeries are on the island of St. John, which rose right up out of the sea in 1796 after a day's roaring and rumbling and thundering. In 1815 there was a similar performance, and from time to time the island has grown larger ever since. One fine day in 1883 there was a great shower of ashes, and, when the clouds had rolled away, two peaks were seen where only one had been, separated by a sandy isthmus. This last was reduced to a fine thread by the earthquake of 1891, and I don't know what new freaks it may have developed by now. I know some friends of mine landed there not long ago and cooked eggs over the jets of steam which gush out of the mountainside. Did you ever hear of using a volcano for a cook-stove?"

"Well, I should say not," said Ted, amused. "These Alaskan volcanoes are great things."

"The one called Makushin has a crater filled with snow in a part of which there is always a cloud of sulphurous smoke. That's making extremes meet, isn't it?"

"Yehl made many strange things," said Kalitan, who had been taking in all this information even more eagerly than Teddy. "He first dwelt on Nass River, and turned two blades of grass into the first man and woman. Then the Thlinkits grew and prospered, till darkness fell upon the earth. A Thlinkit stole the sun and hid it in a box, but Yehl found it and set it so high in the heavens that none could touch it. Then the Thlinkits grew and spread abroad. But a great flood came, and all were swept away save two, who tossed long upon the flood on a raft of logs until Yehl pitied, and carried them to Mt. Edgecomb, where they dwelt until the waters fell."

"Old Kala-kash tells this story, and he says that one of these people, when very old, went down through the crater of the mountain, and, given long life by Yehl, stays there always to hold up the earth out of the water. But the other lives in the crater as the Thunder Bird, Hahtla, whose wing-flap is the thunder and whose glance is the lightning. The osprey is his totem, and his face glares in our blankets and totems."

"I've wondered what that fierce bird was," said Teddy, who was always quite carried away with Kalitan's strange legends.

"Well, what else do we see on the way to Nome, father?"

"The most remarkable thing happening in the Bering Sea is the seal industry, but I do not think we pass near enough to the islands to see any of that. You'd better run about and see the ship now," and the boys needed no second permission.

It was not many days before they knew everybody on board, from captain to deck hands, and were prime favourites with them all. Ted and Kalitan enjoyed every moment. There was always something new to see or hear, and ere they reached their journey's end, they had heard all about seals and sealing, although the famous Pribylov Islands were too far to the west of the vessel's route for them to see them. They sighted the United States revenue cutter which plies about the seal islands to keep off poachers, for no one is allowed to kill seals or to land on this government reservation except from government vessels. The scent of the rookeries, where millions of seals have been killed in the last hundred years, is noticed far out at sea, and often the barking of the animals can be heard by passing vessels.

"Why is sealskin so valuable, father?" asked Ted.

"It has always been admired because it is so warm and soft," replied Mr. Strong. "All the ladies fancy it, and it never seems to go out of fashion. There was a time, when the Pribylov Islands were first discovered, that sealskins were so plentiful that they sold in Alaska for a dollar apiece. Hunters killed so many, killing old and young, that soon there were scarcely any left, so a law was passed by the Russian government forbidding any killing for five years. Since the Americans have owned Alaska they have protected the seals, allowing them to be killed only at certain times, and only male seals from two to four years old are killed. The Indians are always the killers, and are wonderfully swift and clever, never missing a blow and always killing instantly, so that there is almost no suffering."

"How do they know where to find the seals?" asked Ted.

"For half the year the seals swim about the sea, but in May they return to their favourite haunts. In these rookeries families of them herd on the rocks, the male staying at home with his funny little black puppies, while the mother swims about seeking food. The seals are very timid, and will rush into the water at the least strange noise. A story is told that the barking of a little pet dog belonging to a Russian at one of the rookeries lost him a hundred thousand dollars, for the seals took fright and scurried away before any one could say 'Jack Robinson!'"

"Rather an expensive pup!" commented Ted. "But what about the seals, daddy?"

"You seem to think I am an encyclopædia on the seal question," said his father. "There is not much else to tell you."

"How can they manage always to kill the right ones?" demanded Ted.

"The gay bachelor seals herd together away from the rest and sleep at night on the rocks. Early in the morning the Aleuts slip in between them and the herd and drive them slowly to the killing-ground, where they are quickly killed and skinned and the skins taken to the salting-house. The Indians use the flesh and blubber, and the climate is such that before another year the hollow bones are lost in the grass and earth."

"What becomes of the skins after they are salted?"

"They are usually sent to London, where they are prepared for market. The work is all done by hand, which is one reason that they are so expensive. They are first worked in sawdust, cleaned, scraped, washed, shaved, plucked, dyed with a hand-brush from eight to twelve times, washed again and freed from the least speck of grease by a last bath in hot sawdust or sand."

"I don't wonder a sealskin coat costs so much," said Ted, "if they have got to go through all that performance. I wish we could have seen the islands, but I'd hate to see the seals killed. It doesn't seem like hunting just to knock them on the head. It's too much like the stock-yards at home."

"Yes, but it's a satisfaction to know that it's done in the easiest possible way for the animals.

"What a lot you are learning way up here in Alaska, aren't you, son? To-morrow we'll be at Nome, and then your head will be so stuffed with mines and mining that you will forget all about everything else."

"I don't want to forget any of it," said Ted. "It's all bully."

CHAPTER X

IN THE GOLD COUNTRY

A LOW, sandy beach, without a tree to break its level, rows of plain frame-houses, some tents and wooden shanties scattered about, the surf breaking over the shore in splendid foam,—this was Teddy's first impression of Nome. They had sailed over from St. Michael's to see the great gold-fields, and both the boys were full of eagerness to be on land. It seemed, however, as if their desires were not to be realized, for landing at Nome is a difficult matter.

Nome is on the south shore of that part of Alaska known as Seward Peninsula, and it has no harbour. It is on the open seacoast and catches all the fierce storms that sweep northward over Bering Sea. Generally seacoast towns are built in certain spots because there is a harbour, but Nome was not really built, it "jes' growed," for, when gold was found there, the miners sat down to gather the harvest, caring nothing about a harbour.

Ships cannot go within a mile of land, and passengers have to go ashore in small lighters. Sometimes when they arrive, they cannot go ashore at all, but have to wait several days, taking refuge behind a small island ten miles away, lest they drag their anchors and be dashed to pieces on the shore.

There had been a tremendous storm at Nome the day before Ted arrived, and landing was more difficult than usual, but, impatient as the boys were, at last it seemed safe to venture, and the party left the steamer to be put on a rough barge, flat-bottomed and stout, which was hauled by cable to shore until it grounded on the sands. They were then put in a sort of wooden cage, let down by chains from a huge wooden beam, and swung round in the air like the unloading cranes of a great city, over the surf to a high platform on the land.

"Well, this is a new way to land," cried Ted, who had been rather quiet during the performance, and his father thought a trifle frightened. "It's a sort of a balloon ascension, isn't it?"

"It must be rather hard for the miners, who have been waiting weeks for their mail, when the boat can't land her bags at all," said Mr. Strong. "That sometimes happens. From November to May, Nome is cut off from the world by snow and ice. The only news they receive is by the monthly mail when it comes.

"Over at Kronstadt the Russians have ice-breaking boats which keep the Baltic clear enough of ice for navigation, and plow their way through ice fourteen feet thick for two hundred miles. The Nome miners are very anxious for the government to try this ice-boat service at Nome."

"Why did people settle here in such a forlorn place?" asked Ted, as they made their way to the town, which they found anything but civilized. "I like the Indian houses on the island better than this."

"Your island is more picturesque," said Mr. Strong, "but people came here for what they could get.

"In 1898 gold was discovered on Anvil Creek, which runs into Snake River, and this turned people's eyes in the direction of Nome. Miners rushed here and set to work in the gulches inland, but it was not till the summer of 1899 that gold was found on the beach. A soldier from the barracks—you know this is part of a United States Military Reservation—found gold while digging a well near the beach, and an old miner took out $1,200 worth in twenty days. Then a perfect frenzy seized the people. They flocked to Nome from far and near; they camped on the beach in hundreds and staked their claims. Between one and two thousand men were at work on the beach at one time, yet so good-natured were they that no quarrels seem to have occurred. Doctors, lawyers, barkeepers, and all dropped their business and went to rocking, as they call beach-mining."

"'LET'S WATCH THOSE TWO MEN. THEY HAVE EVIDENTLY STAKED A CLAIM TOGETHER.'"

"Oh, dad, let's hurry and go and see it," cried Ted, as they hurried through their dinner at the hotel. "I thought gold came out of deep mines like copper, and had to be melted out or something, but this seems to be different. Do they just walk along the beach and pick it up? I wish I could."

"Well, it's not quite so simple as that," said Mr. Strong, laughing. "We'll go and see, and then you'll understand," and they went down the crooked streets to the sandy beach.

Men were standing about talking and laughing, others working hard. All manner of men were there scattered over the tundra, and Ted became interested in two who were working together in silence.

"What are they doing?" he asked his father. "I can't see how they expect to get anything worth having out of this mess."

"Beach-mining is quite different from any other," said his father. "Let's watch those two men. They have evidently staked a claim together, which means that nobody but these two can work on the ground they have staked out, and that they must share all the gold they find. They came here to prospect, and evidently found a block of ground which suited them. They then dug a prospect hole down two to five feet until they struck 'bedrock,' which happens to be clay around here. They passed through several layers of sand and gravel before reaching this, and these were carefully examined to see how much gold they contained. Upon reaching a layer which seemed to be a good one, the gravel on top was stripped off and thrown aside and the 'pay streak' worked with the rocker."

"What is that?" asked Ted, who was all ears, while Kalitan was taking in everything with his sharp black eyes.

"That arrangement that looks like a square pan on a saw-buck is the rocker. The rockers usually have copper bottoms, and there is a great demand for sheet copper at Nome, but often there is not enough of it, and the miners have been known to cover them with silver coins. That man you are watching has silver dollars in his, about fifty, I should say. It seems extravagant, doesn't it, but he'll take out many times that amount if he has good luck."

The man, who had glanced up at them, smiled at that and said:

"And, if I don't have luck, I'm broke, anyhow, so fifty or sixty plunks won't make much difference. You going to be a miner, youngster?"

"Not this trip," said Ted, with a smile. "Say, I'd like to know how you get the gold out with that."

"At first we used to put a blanket in the rocker, and wash the pay dirt on that. Our prospect hole has water in it, and we can use it over and over. Some of the holes are dry, and there the men have to pack their pay dirt down to the shore and use surf water for washing. Most of our gold is so fine that the blanket didn't stop it, so now we use 'quick.' I reckon you'd call it mercury, but we call it quick. You see, it saves time, and work-time up here is so short, on account of winter setting in so early, that we have to save up our spare minutes and not waste 'em on long words."

Ted grinned cheerfully and asked: "What do you do with the quick?"

"We paint it over the bottom of the rocker, and it acts like a charm and catches every speck of gold that comes its way as the dirt is washed over it. The quick and the gold make a sort of amalgam."

"But how do you get at the gold after it amalgams, or whatever you call it?" asked Ted.

"Sure we fry it in the frying-pan, and it's elegant pancakes it makes," said the man. "See here," and he pulled from his pocket several flat masses that looked like pieces of yellow sponge. "This is pure gold. All the quick has gone off, and this is the real stuff, just as good as money. An ounce will buy sixteen dollars' worth of anything in Nome."

"It looks mighty pretty," said Ted. "Seems to me it's redder than any gold I ever saw."

"It is," said his father. "Nome beach gold is redder and brighter than any other Alaskan gold. I guess I'll have to get you each a piece for a souvenir," and both boys were made happy by the present of a quaintly shaped nugget, bought by Mr. Strong from the very miner who had mined it, which of course added to its value.

"You're gathering quite a lot of souvenirs, Ted," said his father. "It's a great relief that you have not asked me for anything alive yet. I have been expecting a modest request for a Malamute or a Husky pup, or perhaps a pet reindeer to take home, but so far you have been quite moderate in your demands."

"Kalitan never asks for anything," said Ted. "I asked him once why it was, and he said Indian boys never got what they asked for; that sometimes they had things given to them that they hadn't asked for, but, if he asked the Tyee for anything, all he got was 'Good Indian get things for himself,' and he had to go to work to get the thing he wanted. I guess it's a pretty good plan, too, for I notice that I get just as much as I did when I used to tease you for things," Teddy added, sagely.

"Wise boy," said his father. "You're certainly more agreeable to live with. The next thing you are to have is a visit to an Esquimo village, and, if I can find some of the Esquimo carvings, you shall have something to take home to mother. Kalitan, what would you like to remember the Esquimos by?"

Kalitan smiled and replied, simply, "Mukluks."

"What are mukluks?" demanded Ted.

"Esquimo moccasins," said Mr. Strong. "Well, you shall both have a pair, and they are rather pretty things, too, as the Esquimos make them."

CHAPTER XI

AFTERNOON TEA IN AN EGLU

THE Esquimo village was reached across the tundra, and Teddy and Kalitan were much interested in the queer houses. Built for the long winter of six or eight months, when it is impossible to do anything out-of-doors, the eglu seems quite comfortable from the Esquimo point of view, but very strange to their American cousins.

"I thought the Esquimos lived in snow houses," said Ted, as they looked at the queer little huts, and Kalitan exclaimed:

"Huh! Innuit queer Indian!"

"No," said Mr. Strong; "his hut is built by digging a hole about six feet deep and standing logs up side by side around the hole. On the top of these are placed logs which rest even with the ground. Stringers are put across these, and other logs and moss and mud roofed over it, leaving an opening in the middle about two feet square. This is covered with a piece of walrus entrail so thin and transparent that light easily passes through it, and it serves as a window, the only one they have. A smoke-hole is cut through the roof, but there is no door, for the hut is entered through another room built in the same way, fifteen or twenty feet distant, and connected by an underground passage about two feet square with the main room. The entrance-room is entered through a hole in the roof, from which a ladder reaches the bottom of the passage."

"Can we go into a hut?" asked Ted.

"I'll ask that woman cooking over there," said Mr. Strong, as they went up to a woman who was cooking over a peat fire, holding over the coals an old battered skillet in which she was frying fish. She nodded and smiled at the boys, and, as Esquimos are always friendly and hospitable souls, told them to go right into her eglu, which was close by.

They climbed down the ladder, crawled along the narrow passage to where a skin hung before an opening, and, pushing it aside, entered the living-room. Here they found an old man busily engaged in carving a walrus tooth, another sewing mukluks, while a girl was singing a quaint lullaby to a child of two in the corner.

The young girl rose, and, putting the baby down on a pile of skins, spoke to them in good English, saying quietly:

"You are welcome. I am Alalik."

"May we see your wares? We wish to buy," said Mr. Strong, courteously.

"You may see, whether you buy or not," she said, with a smile, which showed a mouth full of even white teeth, and she spread out before them a collection of Esquimo goods. There were all kinds of carvings from walrus tusks, grass baskets, moccasins of walrus hide, stone bowls and cups,parkas made of reindeer skin, and one superb one of bird feathers, ramleikas, and all manner of carved trinkets, the most charming of which, to Ted's eyes, being a tiny oomiak with an Esquimo in it, made to be used as a breast-pin. This he bought for his mother, and a carving of a baby for Judith; while his father made him and Kalitan happy with presents.

"Where did you learn such English?" asked Mr. Strong of Alalik, wondering, too, where she learned her pretty, modest ways, for Esquimo women are commonly free and easy.

"I was for two years at the Mission at Holy Cross," she said. "There I learned much that was good. Then my mother died, and I came home."

She spoke simply, and Mr. Strong wondered what would be the fate of this sweet-faced girl.

"Did you learn to sew from the sisters?" asked Ted, who had been looking at the garments she had made, in which the stitches, though made in skins and sewn with deer sinew, were as even as though done with a machine.

"Oh, no," she said. "We learn that at home. When I was no larger than Zaksriner there, my mother taught me to braid thread from deer and whale sinew, and we must sew very much in winter if we have anything to sell when summer comes. It is very hard to get enough to live. Since the Boston men come, our people waste the summer in idleness, so we have nothing stored for the winter's food. Hundreds die and many sicknesses come upon us. In the village where my people lived, in each house lay the dead of what the Boston men called measles, and there were not left enough living to bury the dead. Only we escaped, and a Black Gown came from the Mission to help, and he took me and Antisarlook, my brother, to the school. The rest came here, where we live very well because there are in the summer, people who buy what we make in the winter."

"How do you get your skins so soft?" asked Ted, feeling the exquisite texture of a bag she had just finished. It was a beautiful bit of work, a tobacco-pouch or "Tee-rum-i-ute," made of reindeer skin, decorated with beads and the soft creamy fur of the ermine in its summer hue.

"We scrape it a very long time and pull and rub," she said. "Plenty of time for patience in winter."

"Your hands are too small and slim. I shouldn't think you could do much with those stiff skins," said Teddy.

Alalik smiled at the compliment, and a little flush crept into the clear olive of her skin. She was clean and neat, and the eglu, though close from being shut up, was neater than most of the Esquimo houses. The bowl filled with seal oil, which served as fire and light, was unlighted, and Alalik's father motioned to her and said something in Innuit, to which she smilingly replied:

"My father wishes you to eat with us," she said, and produced her flint bag. In this were some wads of fibrous material used for wicks. Rolling a piece of this in wood ashes, she held it between her thumb and a flint, struck her steel against the stone, and sparks flew out which lighted the fibre so that it burst into flame. This was thrown into the bowl of oil, and she deftly began preparing tea. She served it in cups of grass, and Ted thought he had never tasted anything nicer than the cup of afternoon tea served in an eglu.

"Alalik, what were you singing as we came in?" asked Ted.

"A song my mother always sang to us," she replied. "It is called 'Ahmi,' and is an Esquimo slumber song."

"Will you sing it now?" asked Mr. Strong, and she smiled in assent and sang the quaint, crooning lullaby of her Esquimo mother—

"The wind blows over the Yukon.

My husband hunts the deer on the Koyukun Mountains,

Ahmi, Ahmi, sleep, little one, wake not.

Long since my husband departed. Why does he wait in the mountains?

Ahmi, Ahmi, sleep, little one, softly.

Where is my own?

Does he lie starving on the hillside? Why does he linger?

37

Comes he not soon, I will seek him among the mountains.

Ahmi, Ahmi, sleep, little one, sleep.

The crow has come laughing.

His beak is red, his eyes glisten, the false one.

'Thanks for a good meal to Kuskokala the Shaman.

On the sharp mountain quietly lies your husband.'

Ahmi, Ahmi, sleep, little one, wake not.

'Twenty deers' tongues tied to the pack on his shoulders;

Not a tongue in his mouth to call to his wife with,

Wolves, foxes, and ravens are fighting for morsels.

Tough and hard are the sinews, not so the child in your bosom.'

Ahmi, Ahmi, sleep, little one, wake not.

Over the mountains slowly staggers the hunter.

Two bucks' thighs on his shoulders with bladders of fat between them.

Twenty deers' tongues in his belt. Go, gather wood, old woman!

Off flew the crow, liar, cheat, and deceiver!

Wake, little sleeper, and call to your father.

He brings you back fat, marrow and venison fresh from the mountain.

Tired and worn, he has carved a toy of the deer's horn,

While he was sitting and waiting long for the deer on the hillside.

Wake, and see the crow hiding himself from the arrow,

Wake, little one, wake, for here is your father."

Thanking Alalik for the quaint song, sung in a sweet, touching voice, they all took their departure, laden with purchases and delighted with their visit.

"But you must not think this is a fair sample of Esquimo hut or Esquimo life," said Mr. Strong to the boys. "These are near enough civilized to show the best side of their race, but theirs must be a terrible existence who are inland or on islands where no one ever comes, and whose only idea of life is a constant struggle for food."

"I think I would rather be an American," remarked Ted, while Kalitan said, briefly:

"I like Thlinkit."

CHAPTER XII

THE SPLENDOUR OF SAGHALIE TYEE

THE tundra was greenish-brown in colour, and looked like a great meadow stretching from the beach, like a new moon, gently upward to the cones of volcanic mountains far away.

The ground, frozen solid all the year, thaws out for a foot or two on the surface during the warm months, and here and there were scattered wild flowers; spring beauties, purple primroses, yellow anemone, and saxifrages bloomed in beauty, and wild honey-bees, gay bumblebees, and fat mosquitoes buzzed and hummed everywhere.

Ted and Kalitan were going to see the reindeer farm at Port Clarence, and, as this was to be their last jaunt in Alaska, they were determined to make the best of it. Next day they were to take ship from Cape Prince of Wales and go straight to Sitka. Here Ted was to start for home, and Mr. Strong was to leave Kalitan at the Mission School for a year's schooling, which, to Kalitan's great delight, was to be a present to him from his American friends.

"Tell us about the reindeer farms, daddy. Have they always been here?" demanded Ted, as they tramped over the tundra, covered with moss, grass, and flowers.

"No," said his father. "They are quite recent arrivals in Alaska. The Esquimos used to live entirely upon the game they killed before the whites came. There were many walruses, which they used for many things; whales, too, they could easily capture before the whalers drove them north, and then they hunted the wild reindeer, until now there are scarcely any left. There was little left for them to eat but small fish, for you see the whites had taken away or destroyed their food supplies.

"One day, in 1891, an American vessel discovered an entire village of Esquimos starving, being reduced to eating their dogs, and it was thought quite time that the government did something for these people whose land they had bought. Finding that people of the same race in Siberia were prosperous and healthy, they sent to investigate conditions, and found that the Siberian Esquimos lived entirely by means of the reindeer. The government decided to start a reindeer farm and see if it would not benefit the natives."

"How does it work?" asked Ted.

"Very well, indeed," said his father. "At first about two hundred animals were brought over, and they increased about fifty per cent. the first year. Everywhere in the arctic region the tundra gives the reindeer the moss he lives on. It is never dry in summer because the frost prevents any underground drainage, and even in winter the animals feed upon it and thrive. There are, it is said, hundreds of thousands of square miles of reindeer moss in Alaska, and reindeer stations have been established in many places, and, as the natives are the only ones allowed to raise them, it seems as if this might be the way found to help the industrious Esquimos to help themselves."

"But if it all belongs to the government, how can it help the natives?" asked Ted.

"Of course they have to be taught the business," said Mr. Strong. "The government brought over some Lapps and Finlanders to care for the deer at first, and these took young Esquimos to train. Each one serves five years as herder, having a certain number of deer set apart for him each year, and at the end of his service goes into business for himself."

"Why, I think that's fine," cried Ted. "Oh, Daddy, what is that? It looks like a queer, tangled up forest, all bare branches in the summer."

"That's a reindeer herd lying down for their noonday rest. What you see are their antlers. How would you like to be in the midst of that forest of branches?" asked Mr. Strong.

"No, thank you," said Teddy, but Kalitan said:

"Reindeer very gentle; they will not hurt unless very much frightened."

"What queer-looking animals they are," said Ted, as they approached nearer. "A sort of a cross between a deer and a cow."

"Perhaps they are more useful than handsome, but I think there is something picturesque about them, especially when hitched to sleds and skimming over the frozen ground."

The farm at Teller was certainly an interesting spot. Teddy saw the deer fed and milked, the Lapland women being experts in that line, and found the herders, in their quaint parkas tied around the waist, and conical caps, scarcely less interesting than the deer. Two funny little Lapp babies he took to ride on a large reindeer, which proceeding did not frighten the babies half so much as did the white boy who put them on the deer. A reindeer was to them an every-day occurrence, but a Boston boy was quite another matter.

"TWO FUNNY LITTLE LAPP BABIES HE TOOK TO RIDE ON A LARGE REINDEER."

Better than the reindeer, however, Teddy and Kalitan liked the draught dogs who hauled the water at the station. A great cask on wheels was pulled by five magnificent dogs, beautiful fellows with bright alert faces.

"They are the most faithful creatures in the world," said Mr. Strong, "devoted to their masters, even though the masters are cruel to them. Reindeer can work all day without a mouthful to eat, living on one meal at night of seven pounds of corn-meal mush, with a pound or so of dried fish cooked into it. On long journeys they can live on dried fish and snow, and five dogs will haul four hundred pounds thirty-five miles a day. They carry the United States mails all over Alaska."

"I should think the dog would be worth more than the reindeer," said Ted.

"Many Alaskan travellers say he is by far the best for travelling, but he cannot feed himself on the tundra, nor can he be eaten himself if necessary. The Jarvis expedition proved the value of the reindeer," said Mr. Strong.

"What was that?" asked Ted.

"Some years ago a whale fleet was caught in the ice near Point Barrow, and in danger of starving to death, and word of this was sent to the government. The President ordered the revenue cutter Bear to go as far north as possible and send a relief party over the ice by sledge with provisions.

"When the Bear could go no farther, her commander landed Lieutenant Jarvis, who was familiar with the region, and a relief party. They were to seek the nearest reindeer station and drive a reindeer herd to the relief of the starving people. The party reached Cape Nome and secured some deer, and the rescue was made, but under such difficulties that it is one of the most heroic stories of the age. These men drove four hundred reindeer over two thousand miles north of the Arctic Circle, over frozen seas and snow-covered mountains, and found the starving sailors, who ate the fresh reindeer meat, which lasted until the ice melted in the spring and set them free."

"I think that was fine," said Ted. "But it seems a little hard on the reindeer, doesn't it, to tramp all that distance just to be eaten?"

"Animals made for man," said Kalitan, briefly.

A golden glory filled the sky, running upwards toward the zenith, spreading there in varying colours from palest yellow to orange and deepest, richest red. Glowing streams of light streamed heavenward like feathery wings, as Ted and Kalitan sailed southward, and Ted exclaimed in wonder: "What is it?"

"The splendour of Saghalie Tyee," said Kalitan, solemnly.

"The Aurora Borealis," said Mr. Strong, "and very fortunate you are to see it. Indeed, Teddy, you seem to have brought good luck, for everything has gone well this trip. Our faces are turned homeward now, but we will have to come again next summer and bring mother and Judith."

"I'll be glad to get home to mother again," said Ted, then noting Kalitan's wistful face, "We'll find you at Sitka and go home with you to the island," and he put his arm affectionately over the Indian boy's shoulder. Kalitan pointed to the sky, whence the splendour was fading, and a flock of birds was skimming southwards.

"From the sky fades the splendour of Saghalie Tyee," he said. "The summer is gone, the birds fly southward. The light goes from me when my White Brother goes with the birds. Unless he return with them, all is dark for Kalitan!"

THE END.